My Mother the Witch

My Mother
the Witch

by Rose Blue

illustrated by Ted Lewin

McGraw-Hill Book Company

New York   St. Louis   San Francisco   Auckland
Bogotá   Düsseldorf   Johannesburg   London   Madrid
Mexico   Montreal   New Delhi   Panama   Paris
São Paulo   Singapore   Sydney   Tokyo   Toronto

Library of Congress Cataloging in Publication Data

Blue, Rose. My mother, the witch.

Summary: In Chatham, Mass., in 1717 10-year-old Betsy feels sick with fear as more and more incidents seem to indicate that her mother is a witch.

[1. Witchcraft—Massachusetts—Fiction. 2. Massachusetts—Social life and customs—Colonial period, ca. 1600–1775—Fiction] I. Lewin, Ted. II. Title.

PZ7.B6248My [Fic] 79-23950

ISBN 0-07-006169-6

1 2 3 4 5 6 7 8 9 BPBP 8 7 6 5 4 3 2 1 0

With sincere appreciation to Mr. Edouard A. Stackpole, Director of the Peter Folger Museum of the Nantucket Historical Association, and to Ms. Louise Hussey, Peter Folger Museum librarian, for their very valuable assistance.

For Carolyn and Debbie and their lovely green-eyed mother.

My Mother the Witch

CHAPTER ONE

"Mama!" Betsy called. "Mama, I'm home." The iron kettle bubbled fragrantly in the kitchen hearth. The pewter standing on the dresser mirrored the fire's flames. But without Mama the house seemed empty. Mama was always there after school, ready to hear about Betsy's day. It was a time Betsy looked forward to. A sharing time she loved.

Betsy walked through the keeping room and the spare bedroom where Mama's loom and spinning wheel stood silent and still. Unhappily she dropped her hornbook and slate on the kitchen table. Then she looked out the back door and smiled with relief. Of course. It was May. The very first signs of spring were warming the winds of Cape Cod. The winter-bare twigs of the red bud tree were taking on a pink glow. Branches had begun to swell just the least bit. And Mama was working in the garden.

I

Betsy had been waiting for Mama to kiss away her worries. The worries that Jennifer Tremaine had planted in her head this morning.

Quickly Betsy ran out back. Then she stopped and watched, remembering the words Papa had so often spoken. "Looking at Margaret working in the garden is always a joy." Mama loved it so. And there seemed to be nothing she couldn't do. Nothing that wouldn't grow at her touch.

Mama was raking the vegetable garden, preparing the earth for spring planting. Hearing Betsy's footsteps on the still-hard patch of earth, Mama turned and waved. Her fair hair shone lighter in the afternoon sun. Her long dark, homespun skirt, pulled up at the waist for gardening, moved around her in the soft sea breeze.

"Betsy," she called. "You're home early."

Betsy ran over to her mother. "No, Mama," she laughed. "I'm a little late." Mama greeted Betsy with a warm hug and kiss.

"The sun seemed warmer up here today." Mama leaned on her rake and looked around her on the hilltop where their house stood, not far from the ocean. "I couldn't wait any longer to get the earth ready for the vegetables. I do forget the time, daughter, when I'm in my garden."

"I know. I can see the vegetables growing now, the corn and squash and beans. They all taste so good, Mama. But I can't wait for the roses and pansies and other flowers."

"It will be a while. But soon we will see the daffodils and lilacs and the flowering fruit trees," Mama said. She started to rake again.

"Do you want me to rake a while, Mama, so that you can rest? There is still time before I do my chores."

"Better still, daughter, you can remove some of the mulch

from the east corner of the garden near the trees. I didn't get to that area yet. It hasn't even been spaded."

"Of course, Mama." Betsy began to pick up the twigs and leaves that had lain on the ground all winter long. Mama had taken the twigs and leaves, raked back in late fall, and spread them evenly over the earth. They had covered the ground like a warm patchwork quilt, protecting it from the snows and chill of the Cape Cod winter. After the mulch was removed Mama would prepare the ground for flower beds. She would rake the earth and she would use fertilizer to help the coming bloom.

Betsy worked slowly. She didn't have her mother's strong hands. Before long, Betsy straightened up. Through the air she could smell the ocean breeze shifting slowly into springtime.

Betsy walked back to her mother. "I took off some of the mulch," she told her.

"And then you grew tired of the task." Mama stopped raking to push some wisps of hair off her forehead. She smiled.

"I'll do some more," Betsy offered.

"No need. Tomorrow is time enough. I'm using fertilizer made from ground-up hooves and horns. It helps the plants to grow. And I always mix in a little blood. Blood is very good." Mama leaned on her rake and shook her head, laughing at herself. "Forgive me, Betsy! You have been home for so long and your mother hasn't even asked about your day. Tell me, did anything special happen?"

Betsy didn't answer for a second. She watched Rosie, her pet chicken, search for grubs near the cow shed.

Mama studied Betsy's face closely. "Is anything troubling you, daughter?" she asked.

"Well, it's about witchcraft."

Mama frowned. "Witchcraft?"

3

"It's just something silly Robin Warner and Jennifer Tremaine were saying in school today." Betsy shrugged.

"And just what silliness is that?"

"The children are saying that hailstones are falling in different parts of Chatham. All of a sudden when nobody expects them."

"Random hailstorms," Mama said. "That often happens at winter's end. What do they have to do with witchcraft?"

"People are saying that they are causing damage in the places where they fall."

"That could happen, I suppose. If the sudden storms are severe enough."

"But, Mama, Jennifer told Robin and me something else." Betsy spoke quickly, rushing to get the words out. "Some families are saying that the hailstorms are the work of witches."

Mama shook her head quickly. She gazed out toward the ocean, her green eyes glittering in the rays of the setting sun. "Witchcraft," she murmured. "Well, some people do believe in witches. It was only twenty-five years ago, in 1692, that there were witchcraft trials in Salem." Mama's voice was soft and far away. "But I can't think of anyone who would have reason to want to cause a rain of hailstones here in Chatham."

"Children are silly," Betsy sniffed primly. "But why would grown-ups tell stories?"

"Well, there are some people who fear witches have strange powers. And of course people are afraid. If hailstones keep falling, they call fall in midsummer. That could ruin crops after all the hard work of spring." Mama frowned. "Maybe it will stop by itself."

Mama put her tools in the cow shed. Then she looked at Betsy and smiled. She put her arm around Betsy and pulled her close. "Now come on along, daughter, let's go inside. I have some cornbread and milk for you."

Betsy walked with her mother, skipping every few steps. Mama paused and broke off a forsythia branch. "We'll take this indoors and put it in water. It will force the bloom." She put her arm around Besty again. "The yellow flower will bring sunshine into our house and give us our own special spring-time."

CHAPTER TWO

Betsy poured some milk from the pitcher for Mama and herself. Mama cut slices of cornbread and handed one to Betsy.
Mama's cornbread was always warm and good. And that's how
it made Betsy feel each time she ate it.

Betsy sat at the wooden kitchen table, watching the smoke
rise from the kettle that simmered on the hearth. She sniffed
deeply.

"That fish stew smells delicious, Mama."

"I hope it's as good as it smells. There are cod, onions, milk,
and some herbs in it."

Mama stretched and sat on the wooden bench beside Betsy.
"It's good to sit for a while after all that gardening. Now, how
did your schoolwork go today?" Mama inquired. "You didn't
mention it."

"Everything was fine. Mistress Blanchard drilled us in spelling. She thinks it helps our reading. We're having a spelling bee tomorrow."

"Oh, yes. Tomorrow is the day. It had slipped my mind."

"I'm very good at spelling," Betsy bragged.

"You have always been good at your studies, daughter," Mama declared. "I remember when you were still a little thing, scarcely able to speak. There you were toddling about, into everything. And next thing we knew you were asking your Papa and me all sorts of questions. Why this, and why that."

Betsy laughed as she cleared the table. "I must have been a nuisance."

"Oh, no," Mama protested. "Your Papa and I had so much fun with you." Mama passed her hand over the top of the empty kitchen chair, caressing the spot where Papa had so often sat. "I'm sure he would be so very proud of you now."

"I truly hope I win the spelling bee tomorrow," Betsy said. "I have been working so hard."

"Well, if you wish it, then I wish it for you." Mama got up and hugged Betsy to her. "But whether or not you win tomorrow, I am still very, very proud of you."

Betsy leaned against Mama. Her mother looked down and touched Betsy's hair thoughtfully. "I haven't cut your hair in some time. It is getting a bit hard to manage."

"Whenever you have time, Mama."

"Now is the best time to do what needs doing," Mama said, and reached for the scissors that were on the dresser. "Come. It won't take long."

Betsy sat on a stool near the window and Mama moved about gracefully, quickly and artfully trimming her hair.

Mama said, "Your hair is such a lovely sunshine blond."

Betsy looked at Mama, her long, fair hair now swept up with amber combs. "Your hair is beautiful, Mama."

"But no longer that pale blond. It was lighter when I was

your age. But then it grew to be a deeper shade." Mama trimmed the sides, near Betsy's face. "You have my blond hair. But you have your father's deep brown eyes. It is a lovely contrast."

Betsy watched her mother as she faced her in the sunset light. Her mother was so beautiful in her plain, brown, white-collared dress. Betsy wished she might grow up to look like her. The brightness of late afternoon sunlight streamed through the window and formed dancing beads of gold on Mama's rich blond hair. The light caught Mama's eyes and made them appear still deeper green. Rays bounced off the necklace Mama wore, the necklace with the green stone that so matched her eyes.

Betsy had often wondered about that necklace. It adorned everything Mama wore. Betsy knew that the necklace was not a gift from Papa because he had told her so. But whenever she asked about it Mama looked away without answering, or spoke of something else.

Mama smoothed Betsy's hair, inspecting it carefully. "There. I think it's just right. I don't want to cut too much. I like it long and graceful."

Betsy got up and stared in the metal mirror. "It's so pretty." She beamed. "Thank you, Mama."

"It is easier when you have a pretty daughter," Mama said. "Now I must go down to the root cellar and get some dried apples. It is nearly supper time."

"I'll set the table," Betsy offered. "Then I'll get the water from the well, and throw more feed to Rosie and the other chickens." Feeding the chickens and getting the eggs from their nests in the cow shed were Betsy's daily chores.

Mama worked very hard in and around the house sewing, spinning, knitting, cooking, and gardening. There was also the

8

cow to be milked, butter to be churned, and cheese to be made. Betsy sometimes thought that Mama worked too hard, but when Betsy spoke her thoughts aloud, Mama just laughed. "I have all the help I need from you," Mama said. "Lilliana does just enough, especially in the autumn helping us make the soap and the candles. I have my own way of doing things. Besides, even though your grandfather's drafts would help pay for it, I could never bear anyone underfoot all the time."

A few families in Chatham had servants who lived in their homes. Lilliana lived with the Bradfords. They had a large family as so many of their neighbors did. Mama had arranged with her friend, Mistress Bradford, to share Lilliana part of the time. "I have no need for anyone all the time. There are only Betsy and me," she had told Mistress Bradford. "And I could never have a stranger under my roof. I value my privacy too greatly."

Mama added potatoes she had pared earlier to the stew, and in a short while it was ready. Mama said the blessing, and Betsy and her mother sat at the maplewood kitchen table, sharing the warmth of the hearth and the comfort of their time together.

"Mmm. The stew is delicious!" Betsy exclaimed.

"I tried a new herb," Mama smiled. "It does give it a different flavor. Your father would like a heartier spice, though. Fish stew was always one of his favorites."

"I remember," Betsy said softly.

Supper had always been a special time. When Papa was not at sea for several days at a time, he had always insisted that the family sit down at the table together. And no matter how late Papa got home from a one-day fishing trip, Mama would always wait and eat with him. Betsy did too, when she was bigger.

"Papa always wanted dinner to be a family time," Betsy said aloud.

Mama reached across the table and took Betsy's hand. "And so it is still."

Betsy looked at the empty third chair. Mama had never removed it though two years had passed since Papa was lost at sea. It stayed there throughout every mealtime, just as it always had, at Papa's place at the table.

"You miss him a lot, don't you, Mama?"

"I do, Betsy. But your father will never be gone from this house. Not really."

Betsy squeezed her mother's hand lovingly. "I miss him too, Mama."

Betsy got up and helped Mama clear the table.

"I can finish here, Betsy," Mama said. "You start studying your spelling. If you want to win tomorrow, then you must be ready." She reached into the kitchen cupboard. "Here, Betsy. Take this bowl of dried apples I moistened. Nibble on them as you study."

Betsy sat at the kitchen table, going over her spelling words. Her mother sat nearby and worked on some mending. The light of the oil lamp replaced the light of sunset as night fell. Betsy kept going over and over her schoolwork until her eyes grew heavy. Then Betsy grew as tired as her eyes. She rose quietly from her chair and fetched her pink flannel nightgown from the peg behind her bedroom door. The early spring night was chill, and she hurried to put it on. Then Betsy brushed her hair. It fell into place so much more easily now that Mama had cut it. When Betsy was ready for sleep she went back to the kitchen to find Mama. No matter how tired Betsy grew, she could never sleep until she had said good night to her mother. Usually, they said their evening prayers together.

Betsy looked inside the neat, clean kitchen. It was spotless and empty. Mama wasn't in the keeping room either: she and Betsy rarely used the family room anymore. Then Betsy walked toward the back of the house and up the stairs. She looked out and stopped short. A heavy fog had drifted in from the sea, but Betsy could see Mama on the roofwalk that surrounded the chimney. Though she longed to run to Mama and hug her, Betsy stayed still. She would have to wait.

Mama stood on the roofwalk, her grass-green woolen robe covering her nightgown. A green silken sash tied at the waist kept the robe wrapped tightly around her. Mama's deep golden hair was brushed loose now, and spilled down her back. The fog blanketed the ocean as it did often in Chatham, but the ocean breeze blew gently, caressing Mama's long hair. Betsy remained quiet. Mama paced the length of the roofwalk, gazing into the foggy night. Betsy knew she was watching and waiting for Papa as she had done so many, many nights.

CHAPTER THREE

Betsy rushed home from school the next day, skipping and running as quickly as she possibly could. Without pausing, she ran up the path to her home. She didn't stop on the hilltop as she usually did when the seashore was not closed in by fog. She was always looking for vessels sailing toward the harbor.

When Betsy burst into the kitchen, Mama was seated at the table, visiting with a neighbor. "Oh, good afternoon, Mistress Bradford," Betsy said politely when she saw the plump, friendly brown-haired woman. "I'm sorry, I didn't know that anyone was here."

"That's quite all right, Betsy." Mistress Bradford smiled. "It's nice to see young people with so much energy. I hope you don't mind sharing your exciting news with me."

"I think I can guess," Mama said. "But I would like the pleasure of hearing it from you."

"I won," Betsy cried happily. "I won the spelling bee."

Mama hugged Betsy. "That's wonderful," she said. "I'm so happy for you."

"I spelled 'catechism'," Betsy boasted. "I was the only one who got it right. And look. I won a new pen as a prize."

"That's lovely," said Mistress Bradford, taking the quill pen in her hand. "And nicely decorated, too. But you deserve such a prize. A smart, hard-working girl should be rewarded."

"Betsy has always been very bright," Mama said proudly. "This prize reminds me of the time she first began school. Her teacher told Paul and me how well Betsy was doing and one night he brought home a special surprise."

"I remember!" Betsy broke in. "All the children had plain wooden hornbooks, with their ABC's on a piece of paper. And Papa gave me a hornbook with my name etched on the back as a decoration. He said it was my prize for writing my name so well."

"You have many good memories of your Paul," Mistress Bradford said gently to Mama.

"He is with me always," Mama answered.

Mistress Bradford stood up stiffly and pulled her brown woolen cloak around her. "Well, I must go now. It was good to see you, Margaret. I do envy your youth. These old bones are giving me nothing but trouble these days."

Mama laughed. "Now, Patricia, you're scarcely older than I am. It's just a touch of rheumatism, that's all. The change of seasons brings it on. The special herb tea I prepared for you will help."

"Well, I enjoyed the tea. It did have a lovely aroma. But I don't know what it can do for my aching bones."

Mama put some tea leaves in a small sack and handed it to Mistress Bradford. "Take this home with you, Patricia, and brew a pot now. Have a cup of tea with supper and drink

13

another just before bedtime. You will find it very relaxing."

Mistress Bradford laughed. "I swear, Margaret. You should be a doctor. Using tea as medicine. You have a rare talent for that remedy. But it does have a smooth taste, and when you have my aches and pains you'll try anything.

Mama walked Mistress Bradford to the door. "Stop by again soon, Patricia, and tell me how my tea worked. You should be walking much more briskly when next you come to visit."

"Betsy," Jennifer Tremaine called as the door opened. "Can you come out and play? We're flying kites down near the ocean."

Betsy looked at her mother. "May I, Mama?"

"Certainly, child. The winner of the spelling bee deserves some playtime. Besides, May is a perfect month for flying kites. I'll get the green and yellow kite that we made together last spring."

Betsy ran happily as the wind played along the sandy shore with the children. The sea breezes flapped around her long homespun skirt, brushed through her hair, and lifted the sturdy homemade kite high up toward the clouds. Betsy laughed and held tight to the kite string.

"It's getting away from me!" she squealed.

"That kite flies better than mine," Jennifer said.

"My mother helped me make it," Betsy replied proudly.

"It flies very high. So does Nancy Bradford's kite." Jennifer laughed. "These kites fly like witches!"

Betsy tossed her head. "Oh, Jennifer. What do you know about witches?"

Jennifer stood up straight as her long dark curls moved with the wind. Her brown eyes were very serious. She put one hand on her hip, trying to look like a grown-up. "I know a lot. My father is a minister, you know."

"Of course I know that, Jennifer. But what does being the Reverend Mr. Tremaine's daughter have to do with witches?"

"My father knows a lot about witchcraft. All ministers study the Bible and try to learn to recognize witchcraft. That's how I know witches can fly. They can do lots of other things too. Like tell the future, heal the sick, talk to the dead, change weather." Jennifer giggled. "And that's what that old witch Hepsibeth Mullins did last night. Changed the weather."

"What do you mean?" Betsy asked uneasily.

"Didn't you hear about it?"

"No. What happened?"

"My father told me about it when I came home from school today," Jennifer said. She tried to make her voice sound very important. "He said that hailstones fell on the cow shed in back of the Bond house last night. They frightened the cow! Mistress Bond told my father the hailstones were big and hard, and they seemed to fall from above as though some evil power were throwing them."

"Oh, Jennifer," Betsy exclaimed impatiently. She waved in greeting as Robin Warner ran to join them. "The Bonds are always saying things like that. I was walking near the harbor with Mama a few weeks ago, and we met Mistress Bond. She sounded silly, talking about warding off the evil eye. Mama just listened. She's too polite to argue with Mistress Bond."

Robin passed his hand over his tousled sandy hair. His blue eyes seemed thoughtful. "Well, maybe Mistress Bond is silly," Robin said. "But Jennifer isn't the only one who believes her. Mistress Bond says she passed Hepsibeth Mullins yesterday afternoon. Hepsibeth Mullins was working in her garden and she looked at Mistress Bond in a funny way. Mistress Bond says she gave her the evil eye and that very night the hailstones fell on the Bond's cow shed."

"But that sounds so silly," Betsy declared.

"Maybe," Robin answered. "But Miss Mullins is strange. Living all alone in that run-down house. No husband. She works in her garden often, like your mother, Betsy. She never has company. And she hardly ever talks to anybody but that cat of hers. Did you ever see that cat?" Robin's blue eyes grew round. "All black with those deep green eyes?"

"It's just a cat," Betsy protested.

"The Bonds say it's a witch cat," Robin insisted. "And they say Mistress Mullins is a witch. And lots of people around here are going to believe them."

When Betsy got home she heard the hum of the spinning wheel. Mama was turning the flax she grew in the garden into thread for cloth. Mama looked up, her hands and feet still working the wheel and treadle.

"Did you have a good time, Betsy?" she asked.

"It was fun flying my kite in the wind. But then Jennifer and Robin started this scary talk." Betsy shuddered.

Mama looked up from her spinning wheel and stopped spinning. "Tell me what they said that you found frightening, daughter." She listened as Betsy repeated the stories Jennifer and Robin had told about the Bond family blaming Hepsibeth Mullins for the hailstones. Mama sighed.

"Poor Hepsibeth Mullins," she said. "Being blamed for a hailstone plague. And she, just a woman alone in the world with no family except a cat. I have not found her unpleasant."

"Do you know her, Mama?"

"Not well. She has quite an interesting garden, and often works in it. All sorts of plants and herbs as I have. I stop to admire it whenever I pass by, and she tells me all about her planting. All you have to do is stop and say a friendly hello, and Mistress Mullins is polite enough."

16

"Then why are the Bonds blaming her for the hailstones, Mama?"

"Well, she is different from other people—the way she lives, the way she has no family or friends. People who are different often have problems." Mama shook her head. "If one is not plain as bread pudding made without spice, one can get into trouble. It's terribly sad."

"What will happen to Mistress Mullins?" Betsy asked.

"Mistress Bond is a loose-tongued woman, and everybody knows it. People will not be inclined to take her loose talk seriously." Mama frowned. "Still, such talk can be serious and dangerous. You are too young to know much about it. But it was just such gossip that began the terrible witch trials of Salem, right here in the Massachusetts Bay Colony."

Mama sat back in her chair and looked far away. "I was only a small child then, but my parents were very upset for years after. The trials were brought about by a group of young girls and a servant woman. One of the ministers of Salem, Reverend Samuel Parris, brought Tituba from Barbados. His nine-year-old niece was one of the girls. They began to act very oddly, barking like dogs, grunting like hogs, having spasms. The Reverend Parris decided they were bewitched.

"The girls accused Tituba, and two other poor, old women of being witches." Mama stopped and thought for a moment.

"Yes, Betsy, that was the beginning of it. 'The reign of terror,' Father called it. Neighbor accused neighbor." Mama shook her head as though to clear it.

"Do you think anything bad will happen to Hepsibeth Mullins, Mama?" Betsy's voice trembled.

"I think the talk will die down, Betsy, and then pass altogether. Mistress Bond's stories are almost never remembered longer than butter takes to melt in July. She is a difficult

17

woman for sensible people to take seriously." Mama ran her hand over the even strands of flaxen thread as her eyes seemed to look far away. "And sensible people remember the horrors of Salem. They will be much afraid to risk those horrors again."

CHAPTER FOUR

Maybe the children were too young to know much of Salem. But the next day at playtime Betsy wondered how many people in Chatham still remembered what Mama had called the horrors of the time.

Betsy and a group of children were playing hopscotch outside Mistress Blanchard's house. Jennifer missed for the third time in a row.

"Oh!" she exclaimed. "If only I were a witch like Hepsibeth Mullins. I could cast spells on the other players and win every game."

Betsy chided her. "Why don't you think about the game and not about making up stories, Jennifer? Then maybe you would win."

"I am not making up stories," Jennifer objected. "My father

says witches do cast spells. They can cast spells on their enemies and even make good things happen to people they like."

"Oh, I see," Betsy said in a teasing voice. "And how can they do that?"

"I'll tell you how. They take a piece of the person's clothing or a lock of hair or nail cuttings. Then they recite a magic poem. That's what my father says. And my father knows more than almost anybody."

Betsy thought for a minute. Then suddenly her curiosity grew stronger. She wanted to know more about the powers of witchcraft.

"Tell me, Jennifer," she demanded. "What else are witches supposed to be able to do?"

"Well, they can make things happen by stirring up witches' brews and potions." Jennifer wrinkled her nose. "They use things like ashes of vipers, lizards, and toads."

"That's disgusting, Jennifer."

"But it's true. They can also use wine, herbs, roots, and even the heart of a dove."

"What else did your father tell you?"

"He says witches wear special good-luck charms to make things happen. It can be a rabbit's foot, a medal, or some kind of jewel. My father says it's called a fetish or an amulet. It has power because there's a spirit inside it."

"You said witches can tell the future. How can they do that?"

"Well, they just have that power. And sometimes they can read the stars. There are lots of other things, too."

Mistress Blanchard waved her hand, signaling the children that playtime was over. Everyone stopped talking and walked quietly inside. Mistress Blanchard heard the lessons of each child in turn. Betsy copied a verse on her slate from Mistress

Blanchard's Psalter. She tried not to listen as Robin's youngest brother started to recite in a loud, sing-song voice:

*"In Adam's fall
We sinned all . . ."*

Some girls embroidered. Other children worked with readers and copybooks. When school was dismissed Betsy gathered her things and set out for home.

"Betsy!" Nancy Bradford called. "Betsy. Wait for me."

Betsy turned and waited for Nancy, who was small, plump, and grey-eyed like her mother. Then Jennifer ran and caught up with her classmates.

"My mother made a new doll for me," said Nancy. "Do you want to come over and play for a while?"

"That would be nice," Betsy answered. "I'll run home and ask Mama."

The Bradfords' fields were next to the Wylers' small farm.

"I'd like to see your new doll, Nancy," Jennifer said.

"You can come along too," Nancy invited her. "We'll all play."

The girls played with Flossie, Nancy's new rag doll. They pretended they were feeding and bathing her. Then they put her to sleep in her birch bark crib.

Lilliana came into the room Nancy shared with her older sisters and walked over to the children. She was dressed as she always was, with a bright red kerchief around her dark curls.

"I have gingerbread cakes," she said. "Fresh and hot. You children must be hungry by this time. It's nice to have hot bread in this weather. It still hasn't warmed up for springtime."

"That's because of that old witch, Hepsibeth Mullins," Jennifer said.

That Jennifer couldn't keep her mouth still even when it was filled with gingerbread cake, Betsy thought. "Jennifer is talking about nothing but witches these days," Betsy complained.

"Well, she hears it in her house," Lilliana observed in her soft, musical voice. "The Reverend Mr. Tremaine knows a lot about witchcraft. And some folks do believe strongly. When I was growing up in the West Indies, I heard lots of stories from my Mama. And there's lots of things in this world that folks don't understand."

"But how can the hailstones be Mistress Mullins' fault?" Nancy asked.

"Well, there's mysteries and secrets we can't be sure of," Lilliana told them. "A witch can be home in bed and out making mischief at the same time. So the people say."

"How, Lilliana?" Betsy asked.

"Witches can be in two places at once," Lilliana replied. "And they can use a familiar. That is a bird or a cat that does the witch's work for them. The animal has special powers and does what the witch sends him to do. Who knows what errand an animal is on in the dark of night?"

"Like that witch cat of Hepsibeth Mullins," Jennifer declared.

"Do you think Mistress Mullins is a witch, Lilliana?" Nancy asked.

"I do not wish to think about such things," Lilliana said. She looked quickly over her shoulder. "And even if I did think of them, I would watch my tongue. I would want others to hold their tongues if someone said I was a witch."

"Who would say that?" Betsy laughed uneasily.

"You never can tell," Lilliana said somberly. "I do spin the witchcraft tales I learned in my childhood. And people can say most anything. Why, everyone around Salem was in danger at one time."

"My mother was telling me about Salem yesterday." Betsy frowned.

"Was it very bad then, Lilliana?" Nancy asked.

"Oh, yes. I lived with a family in a town nearby. We heard stories every day back in 1692," Lilliana said, nodding her head. "Almost every day there was talk of more people being brought to trial in Salem. Even children were put in jail."

"Children!" Betsy exclaimed.

"I heard that lots of people were killed," Nancy said.

"Oh, yes," Lilliana nodded grimly. "There were men, but most were women. Most were hung from the scaffold until they died."

Betsy had been feeling fine. But suddenly she had a terrible stomachache. It was silly to think that hearing talk about witches could upset you, but Betsy had eaten Lilliana's gingerbread cake hundreds of times. She knew it wasn't Lilliana's baking that made her stomach hurt.

Betsy walked home slowly along the seashore. She breathed deeply of the May wind that swept in from the ocean. The breezes near the Wyler house tasted of the sea much of the time. Now, Betsy couldn't get enough of the chill moistness in the salty air.

CHAPTER FIVE

Betsy stood outside the front of her house for a few moments, letting the wind blow through her hair and cool her face. Then she went in. When the door closed behind her, Betsy felt safer and more calm. Her stomachache vanished and she felt no further need for the coolness of the outdoors. She was home now.

"Mama!" she called. "Mama, I'm back."

"In here, dear," Mama said.

Betsy followed the smell of fish stew into the kitchen. The aroma was slightly different than it had been last night. Mama must have tried a different herb.

Mistress Bradford sat at the kitchen table sipping tea. "Oh, good afternoon, Mistress Bradford," Betsy greeted her politely. "I hope you are feeling better today."

"Oh, I'm so much better, Betsy. Thank you. And I do owe it all to your wonderful mother."

"Mama?" Betsy asked in a puzzled voice.

"Oh, yes. I was in such terrible pain," Mistress Bradford confided. "I could barely hold a teacup. But that tea your mother gave me worked wonders. Just like a miracle. That's what it was." Mistress Bradford turned to Mama. "I brewed it just as you said, and drank it before bedtime. Tell me, Margaret, what's in your special tea? Can you give me the recipe?"

Mama smiled and shook her head. "I'm afraid I can't, Patricia. I always have herbs in my garden." Mama pointed to the herbs drying from the kitchen rafters. "And in my kitchen, too. I just use a pinch of this and a little of something else and judge as I work."

"Cooks and their recipes," Mistress Bradford snorted. But her grey eyes twinkled. "They never want to part with their precious secrets. Well, I guess I shall have to come here whenever I have need of your special herb tea."

"And you're always welcome, Patricia," Mama assured her. "By not giving out my secrets, I make sure my friends keep coming to visit me."

Mistress Bradford laughed. "Everyone would visit you anyway, Margaret. You know you're one of the best-liked women in Chatham."

"Why, thank you, Patricia," Mama replied. "That's so very nice to hear."

"And very true. You never have an unkind word to say about anyone. And you're always so willing to help."

"I like to help my neighbors, Patricia," Mama said.

"Well, you certainly did help my poor old bones. That tea cured me. You do have a special talent for healing. Why, I remember when my Nancy fell playing outside. You prepared a special ointment and her cuts and bruises were gone in no time. You do have magic hands."

Betsy shivered suddenly in the comfortable kitchen, but she did not speak.

"Oh, Nancy's scrapes were very slight. Anyone could have kissed them away."

"Well, my pains were far from slight. And after your tea, my hands were so free of pain, I was able to help sew a rag doll for Nancy."

"I just saw the doll, Mistress Bradford," Betsy said. "It's very pretty."

Mama walked over to the iron kettle bubbling on the hearth. She lifted the lid and tasted the stew. "It needs a bit more salt," she said.

Mistress Bradford got up. She took the saltcellar from the table and handed it to Mama. Some salt spilled on the table.

"Thank you, Patricia," Mama said. She shook some salt into the bubbling stew and put the cellar back in place. Then she took a damp cloth and carefully wiped the table.

"I'm sorry about spilling the salt." Mistress Bradford laughed. "But they do say salt keeps witches away."

"I like my table clean," said Mama as she wiped up the last grain of salt.

"Yes. You're a fine housekeeper. I know you are more concerned with neatness than with witches." Mistress Bradford sat down but didn't pause for breath before going on. "Speaking of witches, people are talking of nothing but the Bonds and Hepsibeth Mullins."

"That hailstone business is a nuisance," Mama frowned as she spoke.

"Yes," Mistress Bradford answered. "And so is Mistress Bond."

"I hate to speak ill of my neighbors, but I'm afraid I must agree with you. I do hope that Mistress Bond's accusations are nothing more than a nuisance."

"I know what you mean, Margaret. Talk of witches can grow serious. The people who were tortured, jailed, and killed in Salem are proof of that."

"Those memories must not dim too quickly," said Mama somberly, looking into the fire.

"They won't," Mistress Bradford declared. "People do not take the Bonds and their tongue-wagging very seriously. And even those who are suspicious of Hepsibeth Mullins' strange ways are cautious. Nobody in Chatham is in any rush to make accusations of witchcraft. Salem is still in everyone's mind." Mistress Bradford looked at the hourglass on the dresser. "Oh my." She stood up again and pulled on her cloak. "Time goes so quickly. I must get home and help Lilliana put the finishing touches on supper."

When Mistress Bradford had left, Betsy sat at the kitchen table to copy her lessons. She took the quill pen in her hand but stared out the window. That wasn't like Betsy. She usually kept her mind firmly on her lessons. But now her mind kept wandering and the ache she had felt in her stomach earlier had returned, even in the secure warmth of home. The worried, sick feeling had come upon Betsy when Lilliana and Jennifer had spoken of witches in the Bradford house. And the feeling had returned with Mistress Bradford's visit.

"You do have magic hands," Mistress Bradford had told Mama. Mama was always able to heal, and she was wonderful in the garden. She had herbs in her garden—like Hepsibeth Mullins—and the herbs she grew seemed to have special healing powers. Jennifer and Lilliana had said that witches could heal. That was one of their powers. And witches could heal through the use of witches' brews. Why had Mama smiled so mysteriously and refused to share her recipe for herb tea with Mistress Bradford?

Betsy tried to push away the thought, and then she had another, even more disturbing thought. The night before the spelling bee, Mama had cut Betsy's hair. And Betsy had won. Jennifer said that witches used locks of hair to cast spells for good and evil. What had made the spelling of the word "catechism" pop into Betsy's head that morning?

Betsy tried to go back to copying her lessons. But she could scarcely move the pen. The worry grew heavy in Betsy's heart. Could it be? Was Mama a witch? If she was, she was a good witch. She only used her powers to help others. But if it was true, if Mama really was a witch, what would happen if people learned of her special powers? Betsy would never tell anyone her thoughts. But what if the townspeople began thinking. . . . ?

Could Mama one day be accused of witchcraft, as Hepsibeth Mullins was being? Would some busybody like Mistress Bond spread stories about Mama throughout the village? It was possible. And if the dread day ever came, then Mama might be in great danger. Betsy thought of how the women and children were accused in Salem, and felt sick with fear.

There was no use trying to go on with her lessons. The foolish thoughts had made it impossible for Betsy's mind to return to her schoolwork. Maybe they were just that—foolish thoughts. It must be suppertime. She would go in search of Mama and help set the table before she did her chores. Then she would feel better. She and Mama would eat together, talk together, be together. It would be their special hour, just like every other night.

The kettle still simmered on the hearth. Supper was nearly ready, but not quite.

Betsy left the kitchen to look for Mama. She found her on the roofwalk, in the twilight dusk, looking out to sea. Mama gazed far out over the water, toward the last place where Papa's ship had been seen. Betsy watched her quietly and listened. On a still night, from the roofwalk, she could hear the waves hitting against the rocks on the shore. And she could hear the softness of the milder ocean rhythms between the powerful crashes of the waves.

Betsy listened to the sounds of the sea. Mingled with the whispering waves, she heard the whispering sounds of Mama's gentle voice. Betsy listened apprehensively. She could not make out the words, but there was no doubt that Mama was talking to someone. And there was no one for Mama to talk to as she stood alone, facing the sea. No one but Papa.

Betsy felt cold in the evening air. The Reverend Mr. Tremaine had told Jennifer that witches could talk to the dead. Without realizing it, Betsy groaned.

Mama turned. "Why, Betsy!" she exclaimed. "Have you been standing there and waiting long?"

"No, Mama."

Mama walked over and put her arm around Betsy. "Let's go in and have our supper now, daughter. I think you came to tell me that you are hungry."

Betsy took a deep breath. "Mama," she said, voicing the question she was almost afraid to ask. "Mama, do you talk to Papa?"

Mama drew Betsy nearer. She smiled very slightly in the dim twilight shadows. "In a way, Betsy," she confided gently. "In a way."

CHAPTER SIX

For days Betsy went about her daily tasks, trying to keep her foolish fears tucked safely in the back of her mind. She did her lessons, helped Mama churn butter and made pats of cheese. She drew water from the well, fed the chickens, and visited with her friends. Maybe, she thought one night as she copied her lessons, maybe it was all her imagination.

Papa had told her about imagination. He used to sit Betsy on his knee and tell her sea tales. Sometimes he would spin yarns of mermaids, creatures of the sea, half woman, half fish, who would call to the sailors. Some sailors in the stories Papa told followed the sweet sounds of the mermaids' call and crashed their boats against the rocks.

"Will the mermaids call you next time you go to sea?" Betsy had asked shakily.

Papa had laughed. "No. Of course not. I didn't mean to frighten you. The tales of mermaids are made-up stories. They come from the imagination of people. And very bright people, like my Betsy, often have sharper imaginations. But you must not be frightened by things that are not real."

Betsy copied another line of her lesson, thinking about what Papa had said. Sometimes it wasn't so easy to be sure what was imaginary. Especially when you were ten years old and the grown-ups around you couldn't agree. Betsy wished Papa were around so that she could tell him what was happening. She could tell him of her feelings and of her fears, and he would help. Betsy went to her bedroom. She opened the desk box and took out the precious hornbook Papa had given her. She ran her hand over the cool smoothness of the etched design. Suddenly Betsy missed Papa terribly. And the sense of longing for Papa made Betsy want to be with Mama, with the one person in the world who most shared her loss.

Betsy tenderly put the hornbook away. She went back into the kitchen, where Mama stood banking the fire.

"Come, Betsy," Mama said, and pulled up a wooden bench. "Come keep your mother company."

Betsy sat silently, close to her mother, watching the glowing embers.

"You are not talking, Betsy. But I can tell that what you are not saying is serious."

"I was looking at the hornbook Papa gave me when I was small. And I have been thinking of Papa tonight and remembering."

Mama nodded. "That is nothing to feel sad about. I think of Papa all the time. And it does not always sadden me. In fact, often, it gives me comfort."

"Don't you feel bad when you think of Papa?"

"Oh, no. I have so very many good things to remember."
Mama smiled. "I often remember the wonderful days of our
courtship."

"Tell me about it, Mama," Betsy demanded.

"Of course. A ten-year-old girl is not too young to hear
about romance." Mama laughed. "And your parents were very
romantic."

"You met Papa in Boston, didn't you, Mama?"

"Yes, we were the talk of Boston. The daughter of a wealthy
Boston sea captain and a crew member of one of his cod-fishing
boats. Your father worked for my Papa then before he had his
own ship. And often he would sail from Chatham to Boston."

"Did Grandfather like Papa?" Betsy asked.

"Oh, yes. He liked him very much. It would be hard not to
like your Papa. But what my father did not like was a member
of his crew courting his daughter. He would have preferred
someone wealthier, in a higher position, like that dreary Lind-
say Blair. But your Papa was far from dreary. He was tall,
dark, very adventurous in looks and manner. At last Father let
him come courting."

"Did you stay in Grandpa's house when Papa courted you?"
Betsy asked.

"We always had to sit with the family. The young people sat
whispering to each other through a courting stick. That was a
tube, made of wood, about seven feet long, with a mouthpiece
and an earpiece at each end."

"Did you and Papa really use a courting stick?"

"Yes." Mama giggled. "And the family wished they could
hear some of what we said to each other!"

"Were you and Papa never alone?"

"Oh, yes. Young people will find their ways. I remember the
late autumn nights and the husking bees." Mama's eyes held a

34

dreamy happiness as she remembered aloud. "In late autumn the Indian corn is pulled. Then as you know it is taken to corncribs and stored in husks. The corn shucking would turn into lovely parties. Everybody would come to help shuck and to drink cider and eat baked sweets.

"In Boston the unshucked corn was stacked on the ground and a bonfire was lit. The huskers would work happily. But young people would often leave the light of the crowded bonfires and slip away to a private spot in the light of the moon."

Betsy smiled. "And that's what you and Papa did?"

"Oh, yes. And one November night the moon was full and the stars were lit just for the two of us. The air was lovely and your Papa's lips were filled with gentle talk. And your Papa spoke his most important sweet words that night when he asked me to be his wife."

"Did you say yes right away, Mama?" Betsy asked.

"A young woman is supposed to be coy. But I must admit that I did not even think about my answer for one moment."

"Did Grandmother and Grandfather try to talk you out of marrying?"

"Not so much your grandmother. The women in our family have always been inclined to be romantic. But your grandfather put up a bit of a fight. Still, as strong a man as Father is, he is not strong enough to fight love. He came around in time. Papa and I were married and we came to live in Chatham."

"You must have missed Boston," Betsy said.

"Not really. Oh, our clapboard house is not so elegant as the house of a Boston sea captain. But it never seemed to matter. Home was where your father was. And home was Chatham. Many wonderful things came out of our marriage," Mama said softly. "And the most important was you."

Betsy snuggled closer to her mother.

35

She and Mama were a family. And it was warm and good to sit by the fire. But Betsy remembered when there had been three seated together by the hearth.

Betsy also remembered the evening two years ago when the kettle had simmered with stew and Mama waited supper. Papa had gone fishing for cod to the Georges Banks. He had been due back days ago, and each night Mama kept a kettle simmering. She wanted a good hot soup ready for him when he came in from the chill misty waters. Each night when the hour grew late, and twilight turned to night, Mama paced the roofwalk.

Then that evening John Evans, Papa's best friend, and Adam Bryant, and other fishermen and friends from Chatham had come to the Wyler house, wearing long faces, and holding their hats in their hands. They had come to say that the *Hearty Spirit* had been lost at sea. Their voices were sorrowful and their words tried to comfort Mama. John Evans held Mama in his arms and she wept against his shoulder. Then she stood up straight.

"Come to the table," she invited them cordially. "And let me serve the stew to my friends. You have come a long way to visit me on a cold night, and some hot soup will warm us as we wait for Paul."

A few months later, a group of townspeople had come to call on Mama once again. She had greeted her visitors warmly. She seemed to welcome their company—until she learned of the reason for their visit.

"We want to do something to help the family," the Reverend Mr. Tremaine said. He was a gaunt, stoop-shouldered man with a long chin.

"That's most kind of you," Mama replied. "But we are managing quite well."

"Yes," the Reverend said solemnly. "It is hard for a woman

alone, with but one child. And we admire you greatly. You are truly brave. But we wanted to do something to honor your husband's memory."

Mama frowned. "Paul's memory?"

"Yes," the Reverend Mr. Tremaine had said. "We waited until now to erect a stone bearing Paul Wyler's name. It will be a gift from the whole town to the Captain. A place for you and Betsy to visit."

Betsy had seen such stones in the graveyard at Chatham. They stood as memorials over empty graves, bearing the fishermen's names and the words *Lost at Sea.* Tears filled Betsy's eyes as she turned to look at her mother. Mama turned slowly from the hearth.

"It's generous of you to think of us," she replied. "But Paul's ship has never been found. I see no reason for a memorial when we are certain of nothing."

"I understand your feelings," Mr. Bond said. "But the *Hearty Spirit* is three months overdue, Widow Wyler."

The teacup she was holding shook in Mama's hands. Then she placed it on the table before Mr. Bond and looked straight into his eyes. "I believe you suffered a slip of the tongue, Mr. Bond," she said evenly.

John Evans covered Mama's slender hand with his big one. "Mr. Bond meant no harm, Margaret," he assured her.

"Of course not, John," Mama replied calmly. "I often make errors myself."

Adam Bryant reached across the table. "I think I'll have some more of these molasses cakes, Margaret," he said. "No wonder Paul always boasts about your baking."

From that night onward, nobody in Chatham had ever made any more mention of monuments. When Betsy walked through town with her mother, the men would tip their hats and say,

"Good day, Mistress Wyler." The townspeople were fond of Mama, and they admired the love that kept the heart of Paul Wyler's wife from admitting that she was now his widow. The word "dead" was never used about Papa, not in Mama's presence.

And still, Mama paced the balcony, looking toward the horizon and the Georges Banks.

Two years had come and gone. The wives of three of the fishermen on the *Hearty Spirit* had already remarried. One wedding had taken place only last month.

Betsy wondered how it would be with another man living in her home. The family had been three, and now it was two. Betsy could not imagine another man taking the place of her father.

"Mama," she said softly. "May I ask you something?"

"Of course, Betsy. Anything."

"Do you ever think of a new courtship, Mama? Of a man who might ask you to be his wife?"

Mama waited a moment to answer. "I never think such thoughts, Betsy. Not while I am in your father's house. To me, this is still the home of my husband."

Betsy remembered the long-ago nights when a family of three had sat in front of the fire. She pictured her father, seated close to her mother. She pictured his black hair, his strong face, his deep-set, dark eyes. Betsy watched her mother as the light of the dying fire caught her loose blond hair and cast shadows on her green eyes and the green stone of her necklace.

The picture of Papa seemed so real to Betsy. It almost seemed that he was in the room. For just a moment it almost seemed that the light shining on the necklace had parted the green stone, and placed Papa's picture inside it, like a locket sealed frozen forever. Suddenly Betsy remembered Jennifer's words about the amulet of a witch. "It has power because there's a spirit inside it," she had said. Betsy shivered. Fire did strange things to your eyes.

Betsy told herself that her worries were no more than what Papa called imagination. The end of a hard New England winter would send one's thoughts flying off toward the clouds, like a kite in the freedom of the May wind. Betsy tried to keep her mind clear of thoughts of magic, but Jennifer's constantly rambling tongue did little to help. The preacher's daughter had always had a way of trying to act important. And now she seemed to be in charge of a game of follow-the-leader to the witch.

CHAPTER SEVEN

One foggy morning, a couple of days later, Betsy walked toward school and found not one child in sight.

Betsy left for school early each day. Mistress Blanchard was very stern about children coming late. Usually Betsy would meet Nancy or Jennifer and she would have company on the long walk to school. She began to think that she was late.

Then Betsy heard a whisper. "Get down, Robin. She'll see you through the window." There was no mistaking that voice. It was Jennifer, and she was giving orders. Betsy followed the sounds of Jennifer's command. They were mixed with the noises of children moving clumsily through brush.

Betsy looked around. She found that she was at the edge of Hepsibeth Mullins' garden. Jennifer, Nancy, Robin, and other children were crouched down behind a clump of evergreen shrubs, looking toward the back windows of the old woman's house.

"What are you doing here?" Betsy asked.

"Shhh. Get down, Betsy," Jennifer ordered. "She'll hear you."

"Don't be silly," Betsy answered angrily. "Why are you here, in this garden? My mother said that Hepsibeth Mullins' garden is very interesting. Mistress Mullins works hard in her garden and is very proud of it."

Jennifer giggled. "I'll bet she grows special herbs for her witch's potions."

"Jennifer! Stop that. Whatever else she grows, she plants vegetables to eat. Now why are you in her garden?"

"Don't worry, Betsy," Nancy whispered. "We won't ruin the garden. We're not hurting anything or touching the plants. We didn't even walk on the soil." Nancy pointed directly behind her. "We sneaked in through the slats of that old picket fence."

"Why? And why are you all hiding here in the bushes?"

"We want to watch Mistress Mullins," Robin said. "We want to know what she is doing."

"That's spying!" Betsy exclaimed. "My mother says it's wrong to spy on people. She says people are entitled to their privacy."

"Well, we're just trying to help our neighbors," Jennifer declared importantly. "We want to stop the hailstone curse."

"How are you going to stop hailstones from falling by spying on an old woman?"

"Hepsibeth Mullins is a witch," Jennifer insisted, her eyes flashing. "If we wait, maybe we can hear what charms she recites as she prepares her hailstones. See. The fog is lifting. Maybe we can see her witch's cauldron through the kitchen window. We could see what she puts into the cauldron to make her hailstones." Jennifer lowered her voice. "Maybe she'll even come out here to get some fresh herbs for her brew. Then we can see what she picks from the garden."

"I hope she doesn't get too close," Nancy said in a frightened voice. "If she sees us, she might grab everyone and lock us up inside her house." Nancy shuddered. "We might never be found."

"Shhh! Look," commanded Jennifer. "Look there, through the curtain. You can see, she's moving around in her kitchen."

"Of course she is, Jennifer," Betsy scoffed. "It's morning and she's having her breakfast, just like everybody else."

"Look. She's leaving the kitchen now," Jennifer said. "I can't see her any more. Let's watch the chimney."

"Why?" asked Betsy.

"Because witches come out of the chimney and then fly on their broomsticks."

"Oh, Jennifer." Betsy shook her head.

Jennifer paid no attention to the interruption. "Lilliana said that witches smear themselves with flying ointment first. It makes it easier to get through the chimney and fly. Sometimes they make the ointment from bats' blood, soot, and rust from a bell. Or they use a recipe of lard, herb grease, and oil of clove. Maybe that's what Hepsibeth Mullins was doing in her kitchen."

"Look," Nancy whispered hoarsely. "Look. The front door is opening."

"Maybe the chimney is clogged," Robin said.

Everyone stayed very quiet, as the front door slowly opened. Then Hepsibeth Mullins came out. Her hair flowed loosely about the shoulders of a dark, shapeless gown. Straight out in front of her, she held a large, heavy wooden broom. She walked slowly toward the rear of her house. The children held their breath in the morning stillness. Then a shrill, inhuman voice sounded in the damp silence. Mistress Mullins' black cat yowled noisily as it ran behind its mistress, its green eyes gleaming in the foggy air.

Without a word, the children fled from the garden as though they themselves were flying. Hepsibeth Mullins seemed to see no one, and if she heard the movement of the evergreen shrubs she didn't appear to pay attention. Betsy ran after the group, before looking toward Mistress Mullins. Then she slid behind a shrub.

Mistress Blanchard was standing near the rear entrance of Mistress Mullins' house. She stood watching the group of her pupils running down the path like escaping robbers running for their lives. And she wore a very unhappy frown on her thin pointed face.

Crouching lower, Betsy huddled against the evergreen shrub. She didn't dare move. If she left through the rear picket fence Mistress Blanchard would see her. Jennifer had been the ringleader, but Betsy would be the one caught leaving the Mullins garden. And if she tried to leave through the front of the garden, Mistress Mullins would surely see her.

Holding her breath, Betsy waited. Mistress Blanchard's eyes followed the escaping group. When the children had turned the corner, Mistress Blanchard, still looking serious and very displeased, walked on down the lane that led to the school.

Betsy turned to see if the garden was clear. If Hepsibeth Mullins would go back into her house, or even turn away for a moment, Betsy might be able to leave without being heard or seen. Then she heard her own heart pounding as Mistress Mullins spoke.

43

"Oh, Thomas, I don't know where to start," Hepsibeth
Mullins said.

Betsy allowed herself to breathe. Mistress Mullins wasn't
speaking to her. But nobody else was near, except for the cat.
Thomas, she had said. Of course. Hepsibeth Mullins was talking to the cat.

Jennifer said witches talked to their cats because they used
them as familiars. But this sounded more like a lonely old
woman talking to her pet because there was no one else to listen.

Mistress Mullins shook her broom in the air. Jennifer would
say she was getting ready to fly off to a witches' sabbat or on

an errand of evil mischief. "The broom is free of dust now, Thomas," the old woman said. "I think the place to start would be the kitchen."

Betsy watched as Mistress Mullins went back inside the house, the cat at her heels.

The yard was empty now and the fog had lifted. Betsy moved from her hiding place. She looked up at the sky. Betsy couldn't tell time by reading the position of the sun as Mama could, but she knew for certain that it was terribly late for school, and that Mistress Blanchard would be angry.

Betsy ran as fast as she could. She turned the corner, not slowing down. Then she felt the heel of one shoe catching the hem of her long skirt. A second later, Betsy lay on the ground, her right leg pinned under her. She tried to get up, but the leg was too painful. She sank back down, unable to move.

"Took a little spill, did you, dear?" a man's voice said.

Betsy looked up into the kindly face of William Crawford, who worked in the blacksmith shop. Daniel Baxter, another blacksmith, stood beside him.

"I was running because I was late for school," Betsy sobbed. "And I tripped and fell."

"Well, it's good to be on time for school," Mr. Baxter said. "But not if you break your neck doing it." He and Mr. Crawford bent down, and together the two men gently lifted Betsy to her feet. She took a step, and her right leg buckled.

"Easy, young one," Mr. Crawford said. He looked at Betsy's leg and gently touched and moved it. Then he lifted her into his arms.

"I think we'd best forget about school today," he said. "It's best that we see you right straight home."

Mama opened the door when Mr. Baxter knocked.

"Oh, Mama, it hurts so," Betsy cried when she saw her mother.

"I had to carry her, Mistress Wyler," Mr. Crawford said. "I'm afraid her leg is broken."

Mama beckoned the men to come in. She looked terribly worried.

"I think Betsy will be more comfortable in my room," she said, showing the men the way. "Thank you so much for bringing my daughter home."

The men put Betsy gently down on the bed in Mama's large bedroom.

"We will be on our way now, Mistress Wyler, if there is no more we can do," Mr. Crawford said.

Mr. Baxter, the younger blacksmith, smiled bashfully. "We have to open the shop, Mistress Wyler. Besides, you'll have your hands full with your little girl."

When the men had left, Mama came back into the bedroom. She helped Betsy take off her dress and put on a clean night-gown. Then she touched the leg carefully, moving it very slowly.

Betsy groaned. "Is it broken, Mama? It hurts so much!"

"I am not sure as yet," Mama answered quietly.

She took a basin of water and washed the leg, her touch soft and gentle. Then she went into the kitchen. After a while the house was filled with sweet, pungent smells. Then Mama came back to the bed, carrying a small stone jar and some cloth.

"Just a little freshly brewed ointment," Mama said.

Mama quickly applied the ointment in a poultice. Betsy felt a sensation of warm sunlight flowing deep inside her leg. A pleasant tingling feeling filled the leg and then the pain began to turn to numbness.

"What's in the poultice?" she asked sleepily.

"Just some herbs—wild marigold, wolfsbane root, elder. It's all in knowing how much of what to brew. Then it's strained, and the poultice is ready."

Mama spent the day and all that night at Betsy's bedside. In the dimness of half sleep Betsy felt her mother's gentle, skillful hands changing the poultice, and smelled the rich, hot broth Mama gave her in spoonfuls. Then with the dim light of the betty lamp's smoking wick flickering in the darkness of night, Betsy felt herself sinking into a deeper sleep.

When Betsy woke, morning sunlight filled the room and Mama dozed in a chair beside her bed. Betsy felt her right leg. The pain was gone.

"Mama!" she cried. "Mama! My leg doesn't hurt anymore."

47

Mama moved and stretched gracefully, like a kitten in the early dawn. Her blond hair hung uncombed around her green robe. Her tired green eyes smiled.

"Well, that's good news for the morning," she said. She hugged Betsy tightly. "Now let's see if you can stand."

Betsy got up, her mother supporting her firmly. "Now, take a step," Mama instructed.

Betsy took one step, then another. Soon she was walking briskly around the room as though nothing had happened.

"Mama!" she exclaimed. "My leg is all better. You made it all better. And the men said it was broken."

Mama laughed. "They're blacksmiths. And blacksmiths know a great deal about horses, but little about children."

"But it doesn't hurt at all," Betsy said. "It's like magic."

"Well, there's magic in a mother's kiss," Mama teased, and kissed her.

Betsy remembered the warmth she had felt when Mama touched her leg. She remembered the pain leaving and the healing sleep overtaking her. She remembered Mistress Bradford's words to Mama: "You have magic hands." The light feeling of joy at her mended leg mixed with a heavy sense of worry as she remembered Jennifer's words, "Witches can heal the sick."

"Don't be frightened," Mama told her. "Just walk about as you usually do."

"I'll try, Mama," Betsy said. Mama thought Betsy looked worried because she was concerned about her leg. That expression would have to change, Betsy told herself. Mama must never know of Betsy's fear.

CHAPTER EIGHT

After morning prayers and a relaxing breakfast of cornbread with honey and milk, Mama inspected the cupboards. "We have everything we need for the quilting party next Wednesday. Father sent molasses that he brought from Barbados and we have extra honey, too. Mister Bradford brought flour and cornmeal from the miller. But I need to stop at the cobbler's. My daughter will soon need new shoes."

Mama glanced fondly at Betsy. "It is a fairly sunny Saturday morning. Will the walk be too far, daughter?"

"Oh, no, Mama." Betsy was very positive. "I'll help you carry anything you need."

"There won't be anything to carry. The cobbler won't have the shoes finished for some time."

Betsy saw none of her friends when she took Persistence,

their cow, to their lower field. But there were cries of children and the ba-a-a-as of sheep as they passed the Bradfords' big house and the Warners', which was nearer town. Mama remarked, "It's sheep-shearing time."

Betsy and Mama strolled past the harbor, looking toward the pier where seabirds sailed overhead and keened to one another. None of the fishing boats were in, but Mama observed, "Aren't we fortunate, Betsy, our fishermen friends bring us all the fish we need."

They passed the meeting house and cemetery, and stopped at the small group of shops built around the harbor. There was the Village Tavern and the chandler's, where fishermen could find tackle and nets.

Mama looked at some candles in a window. "They are lovely!" she exclaimed. "But my homemade bayberry candles do just as well."

"Your candles always smell so sweet, Mama," said Betsy. "So does the soap you and Lilliana make. It's always fun gathering the berries with Nancy and Robin and the other children."

"Good morning, Mistress Wyler. And Betsy. We missed you at school yesterday."

Mama turned from the window at the sound of Mistress Blanchard's voice.

Betsy hesitated. She felt dishonest because Mistress Blanchard had not seen her running with the group that had been spying on Hepsibeth Mullins. Because Betsy was not in school, Mistress Blanchard would think she had not been with them.

"I fell on the way to school, Mistress Blanchard," Betsy said finally. "Mr. Crawford and Mr. Baxter had to carry me home."

"It gave me quite a fright, Mistress Blanchard," Mama told her, "seeing my daughter carried home by two of our neighbors."

Mistress Blanchard stared sharply at Betsy, and Betsy felt her face redden. Then a warm smile brightened the teacher's prim features.

"I hope you will be joining us at my home for the quilting bee on Wednesday," said Mama.

"Yes, thank you, Mistress Wyler. I am glad to see Betsy walking so well. I am looking forward to the party. I will be a little late, but I am planning to come right after I dismiss my pupils." She smiled again at Betsy and her mother, pulled the shawl she was wearing more tightly around her thin shoulders, and walked down the road after bidding them a good day.

The cobbler was not busy, and in a short while he had Betsy measured for new shoes. As they headed toward home, Mama and Betsy passed the blacksmith shop.

"Mistress Wyler," William Crawford called.

Betsy and Mama walked into the shop. "This is a pleasant surprise," Daniel Baxter greeted them from the back of the shop with a broad smile on his face. "I didn't think I would see Betsy walking about for a long time."

"Just a bruise," Mama answered. "Nothing that a mother couldn't kiss away."

"Mama stayed up all night taking care of me," Betsy said. "She never went to bed."

"Well, you are very lucky to have such a good mother," William Crawford told her. "And such a skilled nurse." He stepped away from the forge where the fire was blazing and shook his gray head. "I'm glad I was wrong. But I could have sworn that leg was broken."

"I was certain also," Daniel Baxter said.

"Well, Mr. Baxter, you are still a bachelor," Mama laughed. "And Mistress Crawford takes care of the bruises in her family. So perhaps the ailments of youngsters are not familiar to you. Besides, young people heal very quickly."

51

Outside the blacksmith shop, when Mama and Betsy tried to avoid a farmer and his wagon drawn by a pair of oxen, they bumped into Mistress Bond.

"How are you, Mistress Wyler?" Mistress Bond asked. "You are looking well. So is Betsy. And I certainly will be at your quilting bee next week."

Mama waited patiently before speaking. Mistress Bond rambled on without waiting for a reply. Her pale blue eyes moved restlessly as she talked, and her stumpy fingers fluttered from the cap on her head to the knitted shawl around her neck. It was not easy to know when she would pause for breath.

"We are quite well, Mistress Bond. And I hope you are well, too."

"Yes. Well, I would be if I hadn't been so shaken by the hailstones. You heard about them, Mistress Wyler?"

"Yes, such weather disturbances are frightful, I'm sure," Mama said mildly. "We must be grateful that no serious damage was done."

"Yes. But still—" Mistress Bond looked down. "Look at this!" she cried. "Right at my feet. A cast-off horseshoe."

"Yes, Mistress Bond," Mama observed. "Outside the blacksmith shop is not an unusual place to find a horseshoe."

Mistress Bond bent, picked up the horseshoe and offered it to Mama. "Take it, Mistress Wyler," she said. "Iron wards off the devil and witches, you know."

"Thank you, Mistress Bond," Mama said. Betsy could see her mother was trying to keep her voice pleasant, but a frown now slightly shadowed her face. It was difficult to chat with Mistress Bond. "Thank you. But, no. You found it. You keep it."

"Well, I can use it," Mistress Bond said. "After all the trouble we've been having. I feared our Bossie would not give milk,

Mistress Wyler." Her eyes were still for a moment while she stared at Mama. Then she remarked, "I was visiting with Mistress Bradford. She was telling how you helped her aches and pains, Mistress Wyler. Magic hands, she says you have, magic hands."

Betsy almost gasped. She shifted from one foot to another.

Mama replied calmly, "There was no magic. Just tea, brewed from herbs I grew in my garden. I am glad I could help my good friend Mistress Bradford. I know you suffered no serious damage from the hail. I am glad your troubles are few." Mama's frown was growing deeper. Betsy wondered if it was Mistress Bond's talk of witchcraft and hailstones or the brightening sun. Mama added, "I hope that you will have nothing but pleasant news to discuss with us at Wednesday's quilting bee."

CHAPTER NINE

Throughout the day Mama worked on preparations for the quilting bee. Betsy helped prepare the batter for Mama's special molasses cakes. Sunday was meeting day. The time passed quickly, and on Monday morning Betsy rose early and set out for school after finishing her chores and eating her breakfast. She didn't want to risk being late and having to rush. One fall was more than enough for a while.

The morning was foggy, but Betsy heard Nancy Bradford call, "Wait for me," as Betsy passed by her house.

Betsy stopped. She was glad to have company on the way to school.

"Did you hear about what happened to the Warners last night?" Nancy asked in an excited whisper.

"No. All the Warners were at evening service."

"It happened again last night," Nancy confided ominously.

"What happened, Nancy?"

"The hailstones. Robin Warner's house was hit. It will take a while for the Warners to repair the roof shingles. Hailstones fell on the flakes, too. But the men had covered the fish with tarpaulin to protect them from the damp fog."

"I'm glad it wasn't worse," Betsy said.

"Well, the Warners are not too upset. But people will worry about their own houses when the news spreads." Nancy stopped in the path and pointed. "Look. There's Robin now. And some of the other children."

Betsy turned and saw them. Robin Warner, Martha Bond, and, of course, Jennifer. The same group, in the very same place—back in Hepsibeth Mullins' garden. It was as though time had not moved past Friday.

"Jennifer," Betsy said as she and Nancy walked up to the group, "are you playing silly games again? You spent the other morning spying on Hepsibeth Mullins, and all you saw was a woman doing some spring cleaning."

"Well, there's something you don't know," Jennifer retorted importantly. "The Warner house was hit by the hailstone curse last night."

"I do know that some hailstones fell there." Betsy turned to Robin. "And I'm sorry for your family's trouble. But did your people put blame on Mistress Mullins?"

Robin shook his head. "They don't believe in witches. They say such talk is foolish."

"Why are you here, then, Robin?" Nancy asked.

"Jennifer is the minister's daughter. She says it's all Hepsibeth Mullins' fault, and she should know."

"Oh, Robin!" Betsy exclaimed. "Your parents would be angry if they knew you were spying on Mistress Mullins." She

57

looked down on the ground and gasped. A pile of stones lay neatly at Jennifer's feet. "What is this?" she asked in a frightened voice.

"Jennifer said we had to gather some stones," Robin answered. "She said we have to teach Mistress Mullins a lesson."

"That's awful!" Nancy cried. "You can't be thinking of hurting an old woman."

"We won't hurt her," Martha Bond said. "We are just going to throw the stones at her house. We'll hide behind these evergreen shrubs. She'll hear the noise, but she won't see us. She'll be frightened, though, and she'll know the townspeople are aware of what she's doing. Then she may think twice before she ruins any more gardens."

"The townspeople don't think she's doing anything," Nancy objected. "You don't see any grownups here, do you? Now come on, before we're late for school."

Jennifer stood firm. "That old witch has to be stopped before she casts a spell on every house in Chatham. She's the one who's sending the hailstones, and she deserves to have her own house stoned." Jennifer bent, picked up a stone, and took aim toward the weathered shingles of Hepsibeth Mullins' small house. Then suddenly she cried out loudly.

Everyone turned and looked straight at Mistress Blanchard, who held Jennifer's upraised arm in a tight grip. The stone fell from Jennifer's hand. Mistress Blanchard loosened her grasp and stood grimly facing her pupils.

"I noticed children running away from here on Friday morning. I thought I would walk by this morning just in case I might find some of my pupils here again. Now, would any of you tell me who is responsible for this disgraceful behavior?"

Robin swallowed. "We all are, Mistress Blanchard," he

volunteered. "Everyone but Nancy Bradford and Betsy Wyler. They were trying to tell us we were foolish."

"And so you were. At the very least. I am pleased at your honesty, Robin. If nothing else."

"We weren't going to hurt Mistress Mullins," Robin said. "That's the truth. We were just going to throw stones at her house."

"I do believe you, Robin," Mistress Blanchard replied. "But you must realize the seriousness of your actions. First a house is stoned—then perhaps a woman. It was just such behavior that led to the witch hunts of Salem."

"We didn't mean any harm," Robin insisted, hanging his head.

"Maybe not, Robin. But you surely would have been guilty of great harm had your teacher not stopped you." Mistress Blanchard shook her head. "Your parents will be most ashamed."

"I know. They will punish me."

"And so, I fear, must I." Mistress Blanchard paused. "I could take a birch switch to you. And place a whispering stick into the mouths of the ringleaders to quiet them." Mistress Blanchard looked straight at Jennifer when she spoke of the silencing bit placed between the teeth. "But I try to avoid physical punishment. Instead, there will be no playtime until school is over, not for the rest of this year."

Everyone groaned. Spring was nearly here. The children looked forward to playing tag, leapfrog, hopscotch, and London Bridge outdoors. Mistress Blanchard had begun to permit them to play ball and use hoops and marbles. It couldn't be a worse time of the year for such punishment. With school over, they would all be busy with many more chores.

"And that's not all," Mistress Blanchard went on. "Except

59

for Nancy and Betsy, until further notice, you will all spend one hour after school in my company. During that hour you will copy from the Scriptures. St. John, Chapter 8, Verse 7, 'He that is without sin among you, let him cast the first stone.' Day after day, week after week, you will copy that line over and over and over, until such time as its meaning sinks into your heads and your hearts."

"I miss the other children," Nancy told Betsy as they played in front of the Wyler house the following Wednesday.

"I know." Betsy rocked the doll's cradle Nancy had brought with her. "You can't play a good game of tag or hopscotch without more children. It's fun playing together, just the two of us, but not all the time."

"We won't be able to play with anyone else after school for a while. I don't know how long Mistress Blanchard will be keeping the other children."

"We would be with the other children if it weren't for Robin," Betsy said. "But we were punished by not having time for play."

"We didn't do anything," Nancy said. "I don't think it's fair."

Betsy tucked the knitted doll under Flossie's chin. "Well, we were in Mistress Mullins' garden. And we did stay to watch. At least I did. That wasn't right. And we knew the children were spying last week and we didn't tell anyone. We would never tell. But grownups don't understand that about children. So, in a way, Mistress Blanchard is being fair by punishing us."

"I suppose so," Nancy answered.

Betsy looked toward her house. "It's getting late. I'd better go in. Mama might need some help."

"All right," Nancy agreed, walking her friend to the door. "I'll see you at school tomorrow."

The warmth of friendly voices and delicious aromas greeted Betsy as she entered her house. The quilting bee was well under way.

"Hello, dear," Mama greeted her. "Won't you join us? Your sampler isn't nearly finished."

Betsy greeted Mama's guests and passed around molasses cakes and apple cider. Then she sat embroidering the alphabet on her canvas sampler.

"Your sampler is coming along very nicely," Mistress Bradford complimented her.

"Thank you," Betsy answered. "But I'm afraid I work very slowly."

"Well, don't you worry about it, Betsy," Mistress Baxter, the blacksmith's white-haired mother, reassured her. "It takes a long time and a lot of practice to learn needlework. One day your fingers will fly as your mother's do."

"Mama is wonderful at embroidery," Betsy said. She studied the colorful quilt, with its cheerful flower and tree design. It had been pieced, and now the women were sitting together, doing the final stitching. "That quilt is so pretty," she told Mistress Baxter.

"I do like that garden design," said Mistress Tremaine, a thin, delicate-looking woman. She nervously smoothed her plain apron over her homespun dress, which was similar to those of the other women in the room. Then she turned to Mistress Warner. "I am sorry about your house. I hear you fell victim to the curse of the hailstones."

"It was not serious," Robin's mother answered. Robin had

her sandy hair and fair complexion. "We have repaired nearly all the damage."

"Still, to think that that witch, Hepsibeth Mullins, may have cast a spell upon you!" Mistress Bond shrilled in a shocked tone.

"Try some of my gingerbread, Mistress Bond," Mama interrupted sweetly. "And do you remember our little talk when we met this past Saturday? I had hoped to hear only good news at our quilting bee. After all, this is a party."

"Yes, Mistress Wyler," Mistress Bond went on. "But when our homes are being ruined and our children are being unjustly punished, it is not to be taken lightly."

"Well, I'm pleased to say that my house is not ruined. And I'm sorry to say that my son's punishment is well deserved," Mistress Warner said firmly. "What those children did was dreadful and dangerous. I am most grateful that Mistress Blanchard put a stop to it, and I think that she is more than lenient in the form of her punishment."

"I quite agree," Mistress Crawford put in.

"You are being very hard on playful youngsters," Mistress Tremaine protested. "After all, it was just a harmless children's prank."

"A children's prank, perhaps," Mistress Warner said, "but harmless only because of the watchful eye of Mistress Blanchard. We must not forget that just such pranks led to the Salem witchcraft trials. And we must keep watch that Chatham does not let such pranks get out of hand."

"You are right," Mistress Bradford agreed. "And almost everyone in this company agrees with you. Nobody in Chatham is in any rush to make accusations of witchcraft." She looked hard at Mistress Bond. "Or to take idle gossip seriously."

"Well," Mama said soothingly, "if I do not take my stitching more seriously, this quilt will never be finished. And since this is a cheerful occasion, I would appreciate some good news to make my fingers more limber."

"Your fingers are limber enough, Mistress Wyler," Mistress Crawford said. "But I do have some good news."

"Oh. We would be delighted to hear it then."

"I met the Samuels in town yesterday. And Mistress Samuels told me that she is expecting a baby next fall."

"Mistress Samuels?" Mama asked. "Do I know her?"

"Of course. But I suppose you are accustomed to hearing her addressed as Mistress Crenshaw."

Betsy looked at Mama. Her busy fingers stopped working and her needle was poised in midair. Her face wore a serious, thoughtful expression. James Crenshaw had been lost at sea along with Papa on the *Hearty Spirit*. Mistress Crenshaw had remarried months ago.

"A baby," Mama murmured as though she were speaking to herself rather than to Mistress Crawford. "Melissa is having a baby."

"Yes," Mistress Baxter said. "Now, isn't that good news?"

Mama looked down at the quilt and slowly continued with her stitching. "Of course. The coming of a new baby is always the very best kind of news. I will get out some yarn tomorrow. It is not too soon to begin knitting for the little one."

The talk grew more lighthearted as the women went on with their work. When the daylight and refreshments were nearly gone, everyone began to depart. Mama smiled and said good-bye to her guests as each in turn thanked her for a lovely afternoon. As Mistress Baxter and Mistress Crawford were leaving, Mama handed them each a small package.

"Please take these molasses cakes home with you and share them with your menfolk. I am very grateful to both of them for bringing Betsy home to me last week."

"Yes," Mistress Baxter said. "Daniel told me of Betsy's fall. I am glad she is well and that Daniel could help. It is very kind of you to thank him with sweets. I know he will enjoy them."

"He surely will," Mistress Crawford agreed heartily. "And so shall my husband, William. Your molasses cakes are marvelous, and so was everything else about your party. I only regret the looseness of Mistress Bond's unpleasant talk."

"Yes," Mama said. "But it passed quickly, I am glad to say. Still, if such pranks and such talk continue they could lead to many problems and much grief." Mama gazed up at the gray sky. Her face and voice seemed far away as her eyes looked toward the storm clouds, and her fingers absentmindedly touched the green stone resting on her neck.

"I wish this uncertain spring weather would settle," she said fervently. "And that the hailstones would stop. Then all this would be over. I yearn for spring, and I wish for it with all my soul."

When Betsy opened the door next morning, it was as though the winds of winter had been stored away deep inside a chest and replaced by the soft air of spring. The branches of the red bud had swelled overnight and some of the buds had burst, giving way to newborn feathery leaves. Whitish flowers had begun to dot the twigs of the silver bell tree; the shadbush was beginning to be shrouded in white blooms.

The garden appeared to have sprung alive. Forsythia shone more yellow in the sunlight. Buds had appeared more clearly throughout the garden. The daffodils seemed more golden, and the early witch hazel was in bloom.

Spring filled the air at last. Betsy skipped down the path joyously—and then she stopped. Her mother's words came back to her through the whispering breezes. The words Mama had spoken as she touched the green stone of her necklace.

"I yearn for spring, and I wish for it with all my soul."

Was it with the soul of a witch that Mama had wished so ardently for spring? Lilliana had said that witches held power over weather. And spring had come to Chatham, just as Mama had wished only the night before.

Mama had wished for spring so that the clear weather would end the plague of the hailstones, and with it the talk of Hepsibeth Mullins. The random storms would stop now, and so would the gossip about Mistress Mullins being a witch. But would the women remember that Mama had wished so hard for spring that her wishing almost seemed to make it so? And now that attention would leave the house and Mistress Mullins' garden, would people begin to think more about Mama's healing powers and the flying fingers of her magic hands? Would they now begin to wonder and to make remarks like Mistress Bond's? Betsy's steps grew slow and heavy as she plodded to school in the clear morning air.

CHAPTER TEN

That afternoon when Betsy came home after school, milk and cornbread were on the table, and Mama was in the garden. Betsy ate and walked back to Mama, who worked among the new shoots.

"I'll be a while, Betsy dear," Mama told her. "There is more to do now that the garden has begun to awaken. Isn't it wonderful?"

"Yes, Mama. Of course," Betsy answered thoughtfully.

Then she spoke in a more cheerful voice. "Can I do anything?"

"Don't you have any lessons?"

"I do have some, Mama."

"Well, you go ahead with them. I know just what needs doing in the garden, and I can work quickly alone."

"All right, Mama. I'll see you in a little while."

Betsy sat copying her lessons. Mistress Blanchard had grown more strict since the incident of Hepsibeth Mullins. Even with the extra-long day, there was still much to do after class.

When the sand had nearly flowed through the hourglass, Mama came back inside.

"I really enjoyed my garden today," she said. "It's nice to see the results of the work begin to show. Are you nearly finished with your lessons, Betsy?"

"Just about."

Mama walked through the rooms curiously. "Did anybody come while I was out back?" she asked. She seemed to be looking for something.

Betsy shook her head. "No, Mama. Nobody."

"Are you sure? I thought I heard John Evans come by."

"No, Mama. You must have heard some other outdoor noises."

"Perhaps so." Mama looked puzzled. "Did a letter arrive, Betsy?" she asked.

"No. I would remember to tell you if a letter arrived, Mama."

"I could have sworn I heard John's voice. Sometimes you get engrossed in your studies. It's possible you did not hear the door."

"If John Evans knocked at the door or called out, I would have heard. And no letter came while I was here. Were you expecting an important letter, Mama?"

"No, dear. Not really. But you never do know when a letter may arrive that will change your life." Mama laughed. "Well, I guess the spring weather has set me daydreaming."

"I guess so, Mama."

"Now I suppose it's time to stop daydreaming or supper will

not get on the table. Come and help me, daughter. We will have some hasty pudding tonight."

Mama handed Betsy a dish of porridge she had prepared earlier. Betsy carefully poured in molasses and started to stir it.

Later, when supper was ready, Mama stood still in the kitchen. "Did you hear something?"

"No," Betsy said. Then she listened. A knock sounded at the door. It seemed almost as if Mama had heard the knock before it sounded. Betsy rose and went to the door.

John Evans laughed when he saw her surprised face. "It's only your friend John Evans, Betsy. You look as though you had seen a ghost."

"Come in, Mr. Evans," she said in a startled voice. "Mama and I were talking about you earlier. Please come in."

John Evans pulled off his knitted cap and walked into the kitchen. Mama smiled warmly, but she did not seem at all surprised. "John, how nice to see you. It's always a brighter day when you come to call."

"Thank you, Margaret. But your charm can brighten any man's day."

Mama laughed. "You have a smooth tongue. But your flattering words will get you supper. And hasty pudding for dessert."

"Thank you, Margaret. The sea air keeps me hungry. And I accept. I would enjoy some of your delicious hasty pudding."

Mama took his coat and pointed to Papa's empty chair. "Of course, John. Do sit down."

Betsy took the pewter from the dresser and set the table. Mama always used the pewter dishes and porringers for company. As Paul Wyler's young bride, she had brought them from Boston with the candle molds and the bread peel she used to put the cakes in and out of the oven.

Betsy listened quietly while Mama and John Evans talked over the supper table.

He was a dark-haired man, like Betsy's father, and his eyes danced with merriment as he told her mother stories of his voyages and talked of their other friends.

"You are coming from Boston now, John?" Mama asked.

"Yes. We sailed into port and then back to Chatham." Suddenly he exclaimed as he put his spoon down. "I picked up the mail for some of my Chatham friends while I was in Boston." John Evans reached into his pocket. "There was a letter for you, Margaret. I almost forgot my excuse for dropping by."

After John Evans had left, Betsy turned to her mother. "Mama," she asked slowly, "how did you know that John Evans would come?"

Mama shrugged. "How could I know? I suppose it was just that John Evans so often sails between Chatham and Boston and is thoughtful enough to bring us our mail on his way back home."

It was true, Betsy thought. It took a great deal of time for mail to come. And the fishermen sped up delivery by bringing the mail to their friends on the way from port. John Evans did bring mail to Mama. But so did Adam Bryant, just as often, and also Papa's many other fisherman friends.

"But when you came in from the garden you asked if a letter had come." Betsy's voice was puzzled. "How could you know that a letter would arrive?"

"Perhaps I thought a bill of exchange from your grandfather was on its way," Mama answered.

Grandfather helped support Betsy and Mama now that Papa was gone. He sent drafts or bills of exchange regularly. "A draft from Grandfather came just last week," Betsy said.

"Oh, yes. So it did. It may have just slipped my mind."

Betsy said no more. Quietly she began to clear the table, as she tried to clear her mind of the thought that witches were said to foretell the future.

"I can do that, dear," Mama said. "It's later than our usual supper hour, since we did have company. You must be tired. You may go and prepare for bed."

Betsy started to leave the kitchen. Then she turned her head at the sound of paper rustling. Mama sat at the still cluttered kitchen table, looking very serious as she opened the letter from Boston.

When Betsy came down to say good night, Mama again was sitting at the kitchen table. The letter was gone, and the table was cleared now, except for a betty lamp and a nearly empty cup of tea. Mama sat, deep in thought, staring down into the cup. Betsy felt a chill in the mild spring evening. Witches, Lilliana had told her, were able to tell fortunes. And often, they would read their secrets in tea leaves.

Mama looked up. "Betsy, dear. Have you come to say good night?"

Betsy stood still, not answering.

"What is it, dear? Don't you feel sleepy yet?" Mama got up. She poured a cup of milk. "Have some milk before bed. That will help. And you can keep me company for a while. I feel so wide awake that the betty lamp might as well be sunlight."

Sitting beside her mother, and sipping her milk, Betsy began to feel better. Mama was very quiet tonight. She spoke little. Betsy thought Mama's mood might have something to do with the letter from Boston. But since Mama didn't mention the letter, Betsy thought that she should not mention it either. Yet even in silence there was a special closeness between Betsy and Mama. And in less quiet times, Betsy and her mother talked frequently, and shared thoughts and feelings like very close friends.

The fact that Betsy was an only child may have made the friendship between mother and daughter especially close. Now with Papa gone, and the family still smaller, Betsy and Mama spent even more time talking together. As Betsy watched her mother by lamplight, she wondered about the one thing Mama would never discuss. She swallowed hard.

"Mama," she said hesitantly. "Your necklace looks pretty in the lamplight."

"Thank you, dear."

"And the stone matches your eyes." Betsy paused. "Mama, are you ever going to tell me who gave you that necklace?"

Mama looked at Betsy. "I never wanted to speak of it because it was such a painful time. But I think that now you are old enough to understand."

"What happened, Mama?"

"It was long ago, during my childhood in Boston. I remember your grandparents telling me that I would soon have a brother or sister to play with. I was eight years old and the only child." Mama's eyes gazed far away. "I looked forward to a new baby in the house.

"I remember the neighborhood women excitedly coming one night to help with the birth. I remember the voices, and even the baby's first cry. And then the silence and the grim faces of the women. The baby was a little girl, and she did not live."

"Oh, Mama!" Betsy cried. "That's terribly sad."

"Yes. Not only did I lose the sister I was promised, I seemed to have lost a mother as well. My mother, always so cheerful and filled with life, became sickly and saddened and almost never left her bed."

"How dreadful. For Grandmother and for you. I can't imagine what I would do if I didn't have my mother to talk with." Betsy grew cold with fear at the thought.

71

"I have always tried to be there for my daughter," Mama said. "I know what it is like to feel alone."

"Who took care of you?" Betsy asked.

"Your grandfather was often away on voyages. He brought home a West Indies woman, Florinda. She nursed Mama and took care of me. She was gentle and very loving. She mothered me when I most needed a mother. And she taught me a great deal."

"What did she teach you, Mama?"

"She told me of her life in the West Indies, of the tales that were part of her youth. And she taught me to brew many kinds of soothing and healing teas."

"Then that is how you learned to use herbs?"

"Yes," Mama said. "And a great deal more. Florinda remained with us for more than two years. Then your grandparents once again spoke of a child coming. The neighborhood women once again visited our house. And this time there was rejoicing. A healthy son was born."

Betsy smiled. "Uncle Michael."

"Yes. Your Uncle Michael had arrived. And Grandma became her old self once again. Shortly afterwards, Florinda went to work for someone else."

"Didn't she stay on to help with the new baby?"

"No. Your grandmother cared for Michael herself. And I was able to help, too. Your grandfather said there was no further need for Florinda. We did have other servants."

"You must have missed her."

Mama nodded. "Very much. Two years is a long time when you are so young. We had grown very close. And before Florinda left, she gave me a gift." Mama fingered the necklace tenderly. "She said it was a lucky charm and that I must wear it always. Florinda filled an important place in my life during a very difficult time. As she wished, I wear her lucky charm."

"I'm glad you told me that story, Mama," Betsy said softly.

Mama covered Betsy's hand with hers. "Well, as I have said, you are growing up. And now, it's growing late." Softly, Mama blew out the oil lamp. "And you are still young enough to need your sleep for school tomorrow."

Betsy lay awake in her bed, the story Mama had told her whirling round in her mind. Where did Florinda learn the secrets she had told Mama? Were there more secrets the servant had taught her than Mama cared to tell? Were the suspected magic powers of the West Indian woman part of the reason Grandfather had let her go so quickly after Uncle Michael's birth? Betsy wondered. And she wondered about the necklace. Had Florinda given Mama more than a good-luck charm? Did the green stone hold the special powers of its giver?

Betsy got up and walked restlessly about the house.

She was not alone in her restlessness tonight. She found Mama once again on the roofwalk. Her hair was brushed loose, and it shone golden in the moonlight. Mama paced the roofwalk and looked out at the starlit ocean. Betsy watched and listened. The gentle waves murmured softly this night, and so did Mama's voice.

In the morning Betsy woke to hear her mother still pacing the roofwalk. Had it not been for the fact that breakfast was on the table, Betsy might have thought that Mama had been there since last night. Mama still seemed very deep in thought when Betsy left for school.

CHAPTER ELEVEN

After school, playtime was dull without the other children, so Betsy came straight home that day. Mama sat knitting in the family room.

"What do you think of this pale yellow yarn, Betsy?" she asked.

Betsy's face glowed. "I remember last summer, the sunny day you let me help with the dyeing. You and Lilliana dyed the yarn and the cloth that you had woven. It's very pretty, Mama," she said, touching it.

"I think a sweater and cap will make a very nice gift for Melissa's baby," Mama said. "Perhaps you could knit the cap, Betsy."

Mama stood up and put her arm around Betsy's waist. "Come into the kitchen, daughter. While you are having corn pudding and milk, there is something I want to talk over with you."

Betsy sat at the table looking at Mama. Her mother seemed terribly serious. "Is anything wrong, Mama?"

"No, Betsy. But I am seriously considering making a big change in my life. It would mean a great change in your life as well, and I will not do it unless you agree."

"What is it, Mama?"

"You remember the letter John Evans brought from Boston last night?"

Betsy nodded solemnly. "Yes, Mama."

"Well, I want to tell you about it now."

"Did it bring important news?"

"In a way, Betsy." Mama paused. "Medical care in New England has not been the best since the colonists first arrived here. It is improving a great deal, though, especially in the towns. Now, Dr. Wharton, a good friend of your grandfather, has written to me with some unfortunate news. It seems that Mistress Henney, a very popular midwife in Boston, has taken ill. She can no longer work."

"That's too bad, Mama."

"Yes. But there was more to the letter than that, Betsy. Dr. Wharton remembered about my talent for healing. I used to help him out a little before I was married. Now he suggests that I come to Boston and carry on Mistress Henney's work."

"You mean move to Boston, Mama? For good?" Betsy was shocked. She had never been to Boston.

"Yes, Betsy."

"That letter *was* important, Mama," Betsy said. She looked at Mama almost fearfully. "Do you remember before Mr. Evans stopped by yesterday? Do you remember asking if a letter had come? You said 'You never know when a letter may arrive that will change your life.' How did you know that, Mama?"

Mama laughed. "How would I really know that? It was just one of those odd coincidences."

Betsy didn't answer. Mama had seemed so sure when she asked about the letter. Betsy wondered. And again, she wondered about the power of a witch to foretell the future.

"In any case, a letter did come. And if we decide to make the move, it really will change our lives."

"Mama," Betsy asked, "why are you thinking of leaving Chatham now?" Since her marriage, home to Mama had always been this house, the house she had shared with Papa. And still only last night, and again this morning, she had stood, looking out toward the fishing banks.

Mama ran her fingers over the pale yellow yarn on her knitting needle.

"This sweater, Betsy, this baby sweater."

"I don't understand, Mama."

"The day of the quilting bee, Mistress Crawford brought good news. Remember, she told me that Mistress Crenshaw was having a new baby? Only now her name was Melissa Samuels. Mistress Samuels." Mama looked at Betsy and a film of tears covered her green eyes. "James Crenshaw was with Papa on the last fishing trip of the *Hearty Spirit*. And now his wife Melissa has another husband, and soon another baby."

Betsy nodded and reached across the table for her mother's hand. "I understand, Mama," she said softly.

"You are very wise for ten years old, dear." Mama swallowed the tears, but her voice still quavered. "Betsy, the neighbors have offered to put up a gravestone for your father. So, too, have our friends and relatives in Boston. And I have always thanked them and refused. But now I have been thinking. A gravestone in the burial ground here in Chatham would be nice. Do you think that would be a good idea?"

Before, Mama had not been able to bring herself to permit a stone in the graveyard. But now it would serve as a token of respect for Papa's memory.

Betsy squeezed her mother's hand. "Yes, Mama. And I think Papa would like the idea too."

Mama took a deep breath. "So do I, Betsy. And, Betsy, the suggestion Dr. Wharton made to me is a good one. I would earn some money, and I would not need as much help for our support from your grandfather.

"And midwifery is rewarding in many ways. It is a good feeling when a baby is born in an easy birth. And it is an even better feeling when the birth is difficult and you are able to help. Dr. Wharton would train me to assume Mistress Henney's duties. He and I have a great deal of respect for each other. He is also aware of my knowledge of herbal medicine. His suggestion is a good one. And I am certain that Papa would want me to take it."

Mama seemed so sure of Papa's feelings. She had spent most of the night on the roofwalk. Betsy had heard her voice in the wind, talking to Papa. Had the ocean winds carried Papa's voice back to Mama? Had his answer come on the ocean waves?

"Is it what you want, Mama?" Betsy asked.

"There is really no future for me here in Chatham," Mama answered.

Betsy thought of Mama's future, and of Mistress Samuels, and she suddenly grew very frightened. Mistress Crenshaw was Mistress Samuels now. Lydia Crenshaw had a stepfather now. And soon she would have to share her mother with a new baby. Betsy pictured herself in Lydia Crenshaw's place and her stomach hurt.

John Evans had given her mother many fond glances last night while they talked. The young blacksmith, Daniel Baxter, always acted shy when he saw Mama. There were several other unmarried men in Chatham. What about Boston? Betsy wondered.

"Mama," Betsy said. "Do you remember telling me of your courtship?"

Mama's sober look vanished. Her eyes twinkled. "I surely do."

"And when I asked you if you might let another man come courting you said, 'Not while I am in your father's house'."

"And now you are wondering what will happen if I am no longer in your father's house?"

Betsy nodded, not daring to speak.

"The future stretches too far to see, Betsy. But for now, and for any future that I can see, I can see no other man in my life. I do not look unkindly on Melissa, or on any woman who chooses to take a second husband. After all, widows are expected to remarry, daughter." She paused and shook her head. "I am still in love with your Papa. Though I may no longer be in his house, your father will still be in my heart."

Betsy felt the tears on her cheeks. "I hope I meet a man I love that much some day, Mama."

"I'm sure you will. You are very loving, and you will be deeply loved in turn. But your mother has a long time to worry about a son-in-law. Now we have a more immediate decision to make. How do you feel about moving to Boston?"

Betsy thought about Chatham and all her friends here. Then she thought of the gossip of witches. And the day Mistress Bond had stared at Mama and remarked: "Magic hands, she says you have, magic hands." She would miss Nancy, Robin, and her classmates. She would miss the town where she had lived all her life, the house where Papa had cared for her, played with her, told stories of the sea to her, and loved her. But she wouldn't miss the fear she had been having for Mama. There would be love in Boston, too. There would be Mama, Grandmother, and Grandfather. Mama wouldn't be alone, and the memories of Papa's love would travel anywhere.

"I think you would make a wonderful midwife, Mama. And I think if you want to work in Boston, then we should go."

"But what about your friends, dear? Won't you miss them?"

"Yes, Mama. But I can make new friends."

"I'm sure you can. This is your last year of school in Chatham. Perhaps you might study art or music in Boston. You know, Betsy, this will make your grandparents very happy. They have never seen you, and they have been urging me to move back to Boston for nearly two years. And now that your Uncle Michael is married and in a house of his own, your grandparents say they are lonely in that big house. I know Grandmother will be glad to take care of you while I am working."

"And Uncle Michael lives nearby too," Betsy said. "It will be nice to have a bigger family."

"Yes." Mama laughed. "But I better watch to see that they do not spoil you."

Betsy smiled happily.

"I know I will enjoy midwifery." Mama's eyes looked far away. "You know, Betsy, it would be nice to be a doctor, like Dr. Wharton."

"If women could be doctors, you would be a very good one, Mama."

"Some day," Mama said in a sure voice. "Some day women will be doctors."

"Why do you say that, Mama?" Betsy asked.

"Not in my time," Mama said firmly. "But one day we will, I just know it."

Later that evening, as she sat copying her lessons, Betsy worriedly tried to picture Boston. Mama had often talked of her home and school. It would be different now. Mama hadn't been there for more than ten years. But her family would surround her. Besides, though she might be leaving Chatham, John Evans and his other fisherman friends made frequent stops in the Boston port, and John Evans would surely be coming to call. It would not take long for Boston to seem like home. And for Mama, the move was an important one. She would be going on with her life, and time, like sand in an hourglass broken and repaired, would once again flow freely.

After supper, Betsy and her mother sat beside the fire that warmed the chill of evening. Even in spring the moist ocean air brought coolness at nightfall.

"I wrote to Dr. Wharton," Mama said. "And told him I would be glad to accept his suggestion."

"That's good, Mama," Betsy said. "He will be happy to know you are coming."

"I hope he will, Betsy. And because the mails are so terribly slow, I shall give the letter to John Evans. He should be in Boston by week's end."

"Will we be moving soon, Mama?" Betsy asked.

Mama nodded. "Another midwife will be needed as soon as possible."

"Then we will leave before summer," Betsy said.

"Much before. Spring is my favorite time of year. It is so lovely to see life blooming after the long, barren months of winter. But spring will be delightful in Boston, and summer, too. I always remember the large, lovely garden surrounding your grandparents' house. It will be well under way by the time we get there. But I hope to make a garden of my own. And until our house in Chatham is sold I hope the Bradfords and our other neighbors will take care of Persistence and the chickens and tend my garden."

"I'm sure they will, Mama," Betsy said.

"Yes. I worked so hard on this garden. And I shall have to depend on my neighbors to watch after it. I can't be in two places at once."

If you were a witch you could! The words formed deep inside Betsy's mind. But she did not allow the thought to pass her lips. Instead she said, "Spring should be lovely in Boston. It will be nice to spend it with Grandmother and Grandfather."

"Yes. It will be a warm family time. And our friends in Chatham will enjoy the season too. Now that the witch scare has ended with winter."

"I am glad the talk about Hepsibeth Mullins has stopped," Betsy said. She looked at her mother. Mama's beautiful face glowed with contentment in the red-gold warmth of the flame. "But there is no such thing as witches, is there?"

"Well, some believe in them," Mama said. "And some say they are only imagination."

"Papa used to tell me about imagination when he told his stories of the sea," Betsy said. Her eyes wandered to the green stone of mother's necklace. "And sometimes I'd wonder."

"Yes. Imagination is a powerful force." Mama rose and banked the fire. Her golden hair and green eyes shone in the dimly flickering flame. "And sometimes by the firelight, candlelight, or dream light of nighttime, it is hard to know what is real."

Rose Blue is the author of more than fourteen books for children, including *A Quiet Place* and *Grandma Didn't Wave Back*. *Cold Rain on the Water*, published by McGraw-Hill, was selected by the National Council for the Social Studies and the Children's Book Council as a Notable Children's Trade Book in the Social Studies for 1979. Ms. Blue has also written numerous short stories.

The author lives in Brooklyn, New York.

Ted Lewin was born and raised in Buffalo, New York. He earned a degree in illustration at Pratt Institute in Brooklyn. To date, he illustrated over fifty books for children, and he wrote the text and drew the pictures for three books in a nature series. In addition, his artwork has appeared in many magazines and periodicals. *My Mother the Witch* is the first book the artist has illustrated for McGraw-Hill.

Mr. Lewin and his wife Betsy live in a Brooklyn brownstone, which they renovated themselves.